A Wearable Art Show

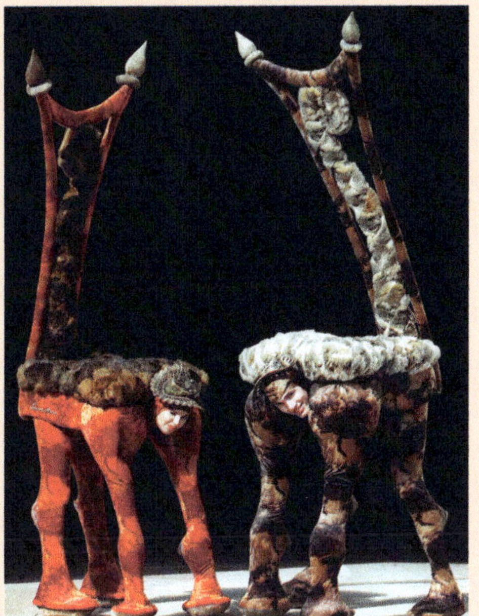

Superminx was designed by Simon Hames, New Zealand

My sincere thanks to the team at the World of WearableArt in Nelson, New Zealand, for their time, information, images and enthusiasm for this book.

Dear Reader

I attended my first World of WearableArt (WOW) Show in 2008 and loved it! The name of the show combines two words together into "WearableArt". It describes an event that brings the worlds of art and fashion together. That night, I knew I had to write about this spectacular show and share the special experience with you.

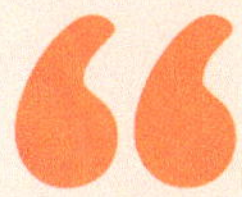

I HAD TO WRITE ABOUT THIS SPECTACULAR SHOW AND SHARE THE SPECIAL EXPERIENCE WITH YOU.

My favourite job was deciding which of the hundreds of creative garments to feature in this book. I hope you like them! More garments can be seen on the WOW website.

I hope that you enjoy reading about the World of WearableArt Awards Show as much as I enjoyed writing about it!

Sharon Parsons

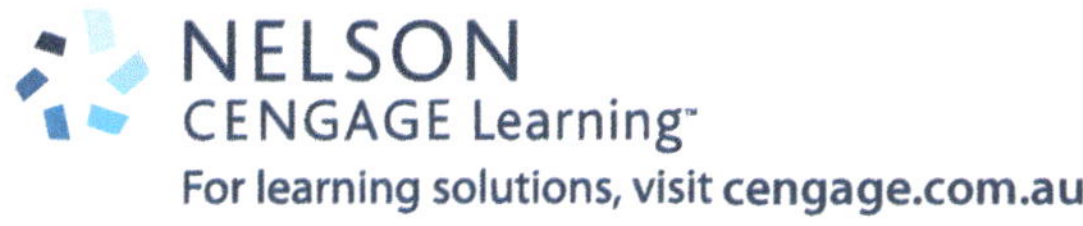

Contents

A Wearable Art Show

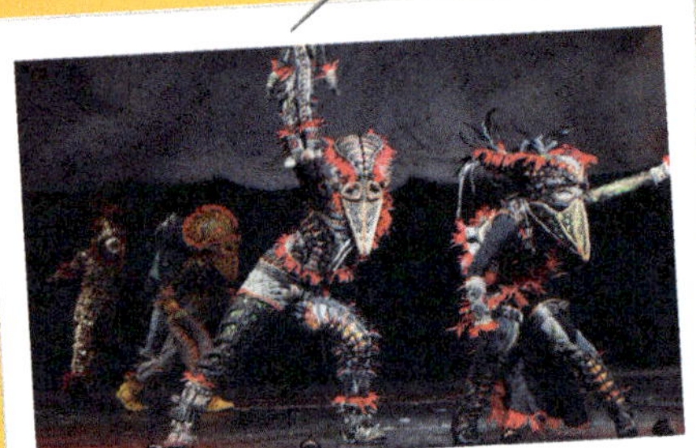

Punk Bird Family, *Sean Purucker, USA*

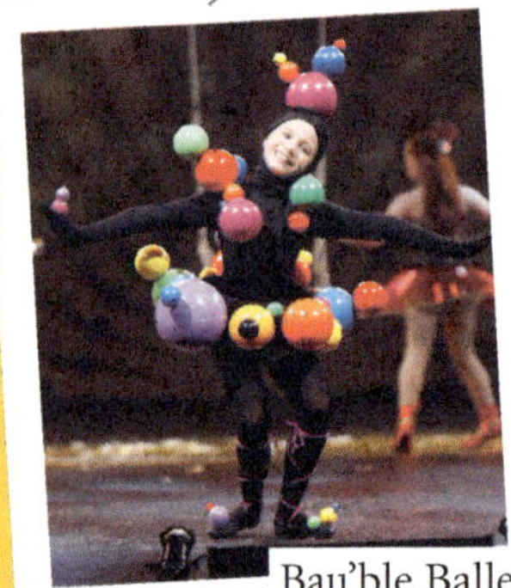

Bau'ble Ballerina, *Amy Craven, New Zealand*

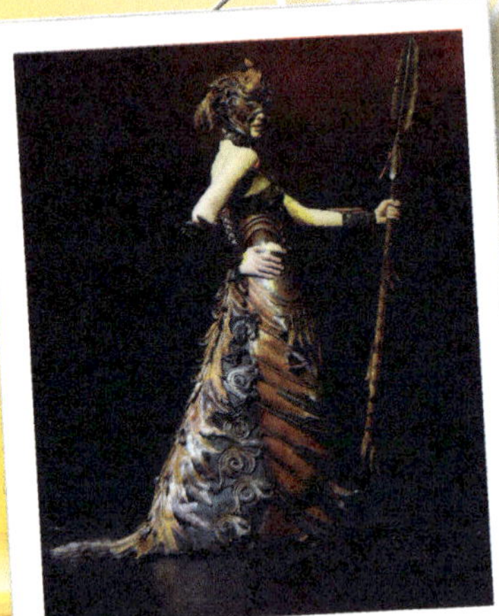

Ornitho-Maia, *Nadine Jaggi, New Zealand*

page 14

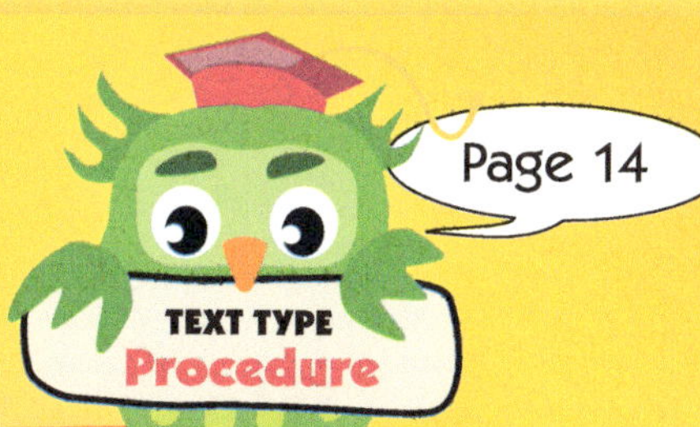

5 Claire Wins WOW Awards

Claire Prebble entered her first WOW garment at eight years of age. She was the youngest designer to win the highest WOW award.

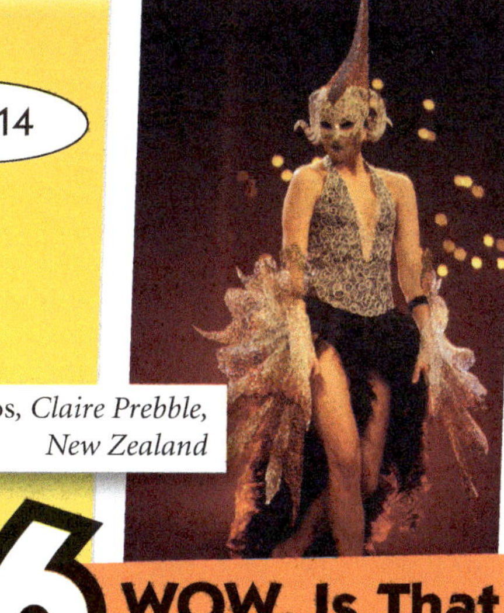

Eos, *Claire Prebble, New Zealand*

page 18

6 WOW, Is That an Illusion?

Turn off the lights to see colourful, illuminating garments dance around the WOW stage.

page 20

7 WOW for the Children

Designers create colourful and fun garments for the children's section of the competition.

page 22

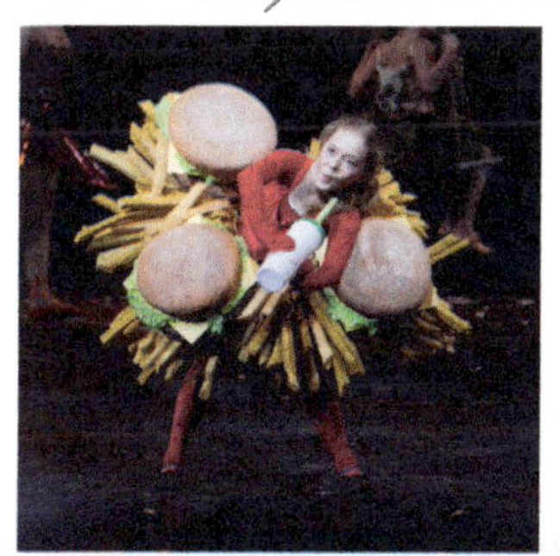

Tu Tu Much, *Ann Skelly, New Zealand*

8 More WOW Winners

A carpenter from Alaska wins a Supreme Award for his wooden ball gown.

1 What Is the WOW Show?

WOW Is the **"World of WearableArt"**

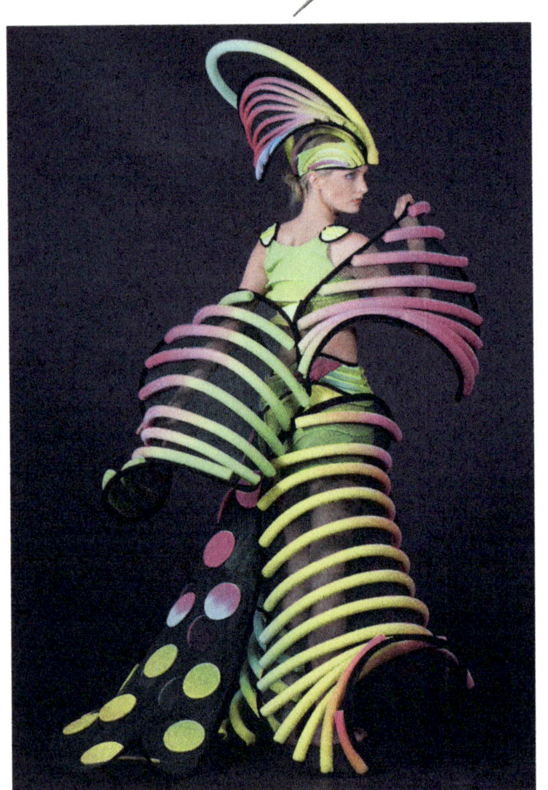

Fluoroessence *by Susan Holmes, New Zealand was a finalist in the Shape It section.*

The World Of WearableArt (WOW) is one of the most unique shows you will ever see!

A new WOW show is performed every year in Wellington, New Zealand. Over 40 000 people from around the world attend the WOW shows each year.

> "IT'S A SHOW WHERE ART AND THE HUMAN FORM COME TOGETHER IN STUNNING LIGHTING, DANCE, DRAMA AND SOUNDSCAPES."
>
> SUZIE MONCRIEFF, WOW Founder

WOW Competition

Hundreds of designers from around the world enter their garments in the WOW competition. It is a great honour to be a finalist and an even greater honour to win.

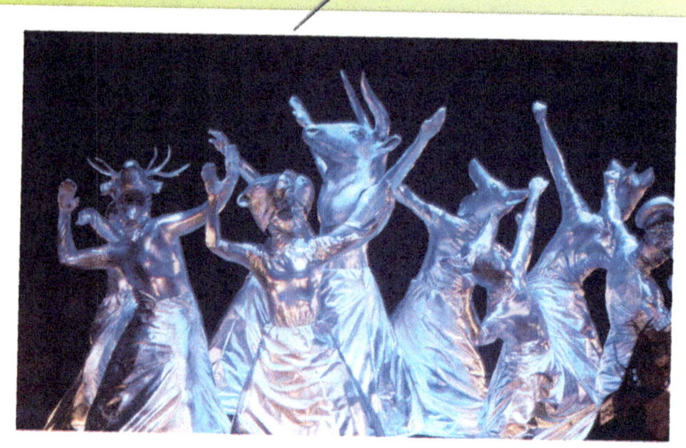

onstage performers at a WOW show

Suzie's Dream

As an artist, Suzie Moncrieff, WOW Founder, wanted to create something in art with a wow factor!

In 1987, Suzie did just that! She created the first World of WearableArt Awards Show and around 200 people attended. Year after year, the WOW shows have became more and more successful.

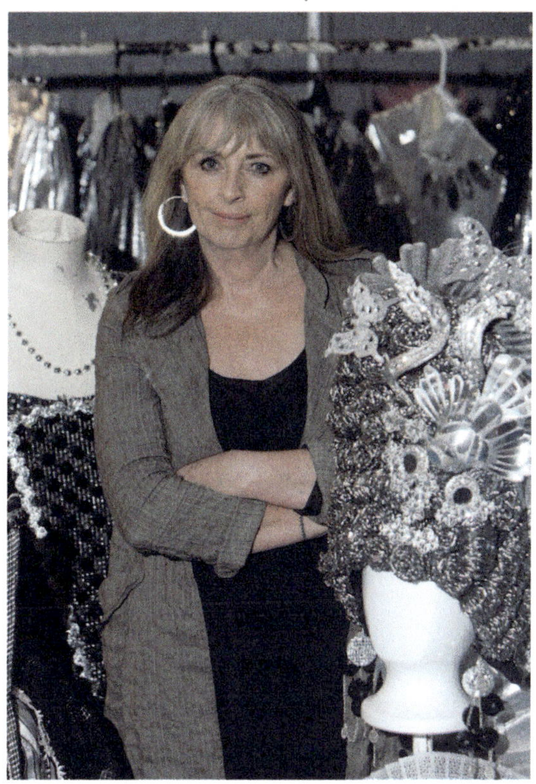

Suzie Moncrieff with a WOW prop garment

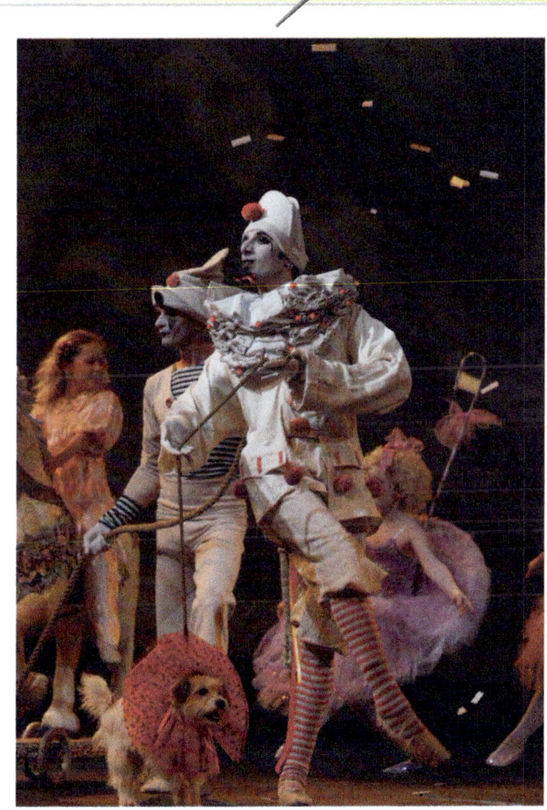

Onstage performers create stories through dance and music when the finalists' garments are modelled.

Arts

Suzie Was a Sculptor

Before the WOW shows, Suzie was a sculptor. While working in an art gallery, Suzie got the idea for the WOW shows.
Suzie says, "I wanted to take art off the wall and adorn the body with art in wildly wonderful ways."

2 WOW, What a Year!

From **October** to **October**

Many people work together to produce each new WOW show. It takes almost a year to get ready. So the WOW team get started in October to prepare for the show in late September of the following year.

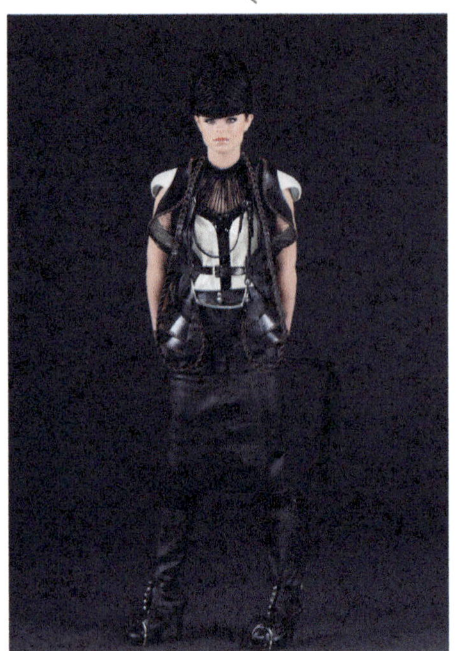

Saddle Up *was designed by Mary Wing To, United Kingdom.*

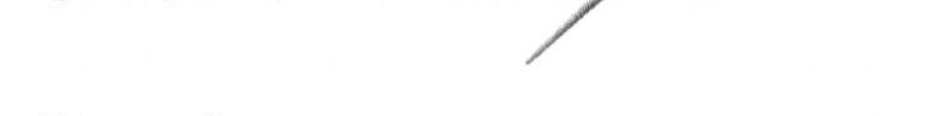

October

Work begins by deciding the new themes for each of the seven competition sections. The WOW team also brainstorms ideas on how to create a spectacular show for next September.

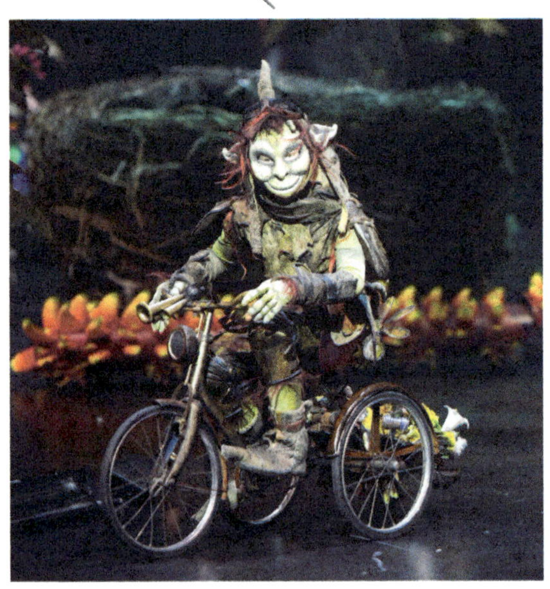

Nilbog the Garden Goblin *was designed by Bronwen Pattison, New Zealand.*

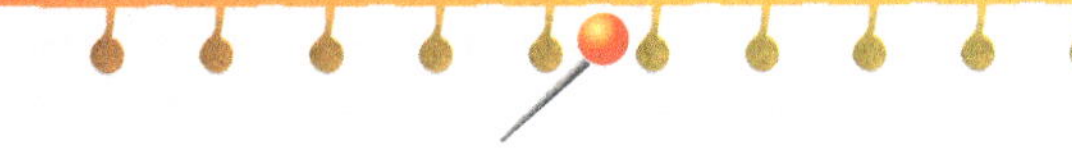

November

Garment entry kits are produced early as the designers' garments can take many months to design and make.

December to June

This is a busy time for the marketing team as they work on the website, tickets, brochures, posters and much more.

WOW Founder, Suzie Moncrieff, and the scripting team work on the new show's script. Then, teams of creative people work with the script team on many jobs. Those people include the artistic director, the production manager, the set designer and the costume designer.

TICKETS

From February about 40 000 tickets go on sale via the Internet. They sell fast!

The WOW Script

The script describes the characters, dancers, models, music, lighting, costumes, stage sets and choreography needed for the seven sections in the competition: Children, Illumination Illusion, Creative Excellence, Man Unleashed, Open, South Pacific and Avant-Garde.

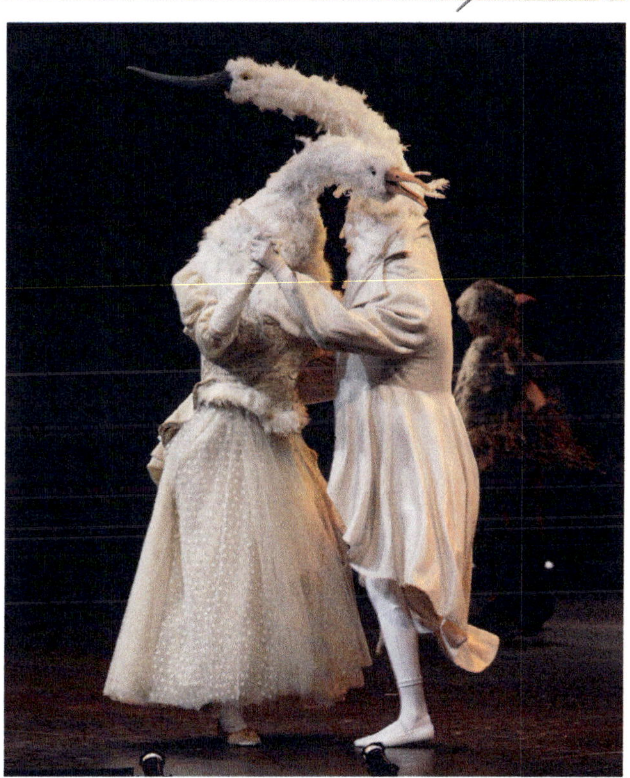

Duck characters dancing onstage during the children's section of the competition.

AUDITIONS

In June, auditions are held for models, dancers and actors. WOW also auditions children aged between 9 and 13 years old to model garments in the children's section.

July to September

Work continues on the production and design of the new WOW show.

The judging of designers' garments starts in July and the final decisions are made on the dress-rehearsal night in September. Judges like to see how the garments look on stage with lights, music and dance!

At the end of September, the judges announce the winners and the first of ten shows is performed to excited audiences.

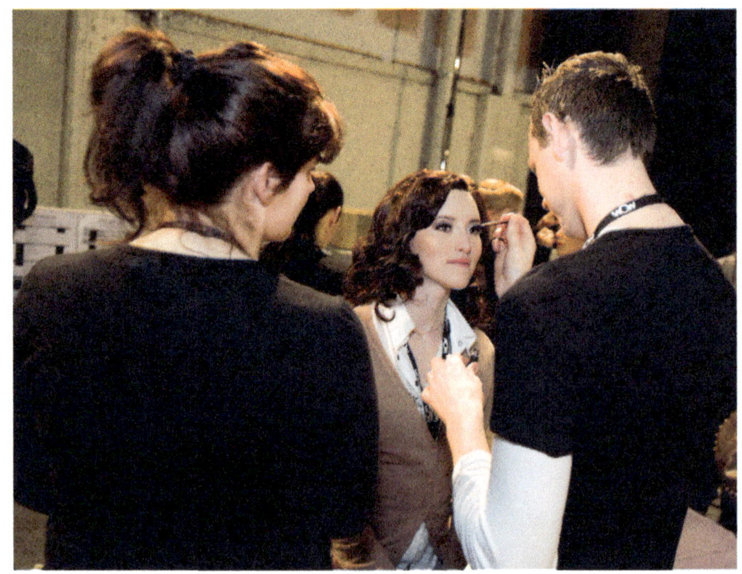

backstage on dress-rehearsal night

GARMENTS

In August, the garments are shipped from Nelson to Wellington. When they are unpacked, the garments are fitted onto models so the rehearsals can begin!

WOW JUDGES

Suzie Moncrieff is assisted by two guest judges who have fashion and arts design experience.

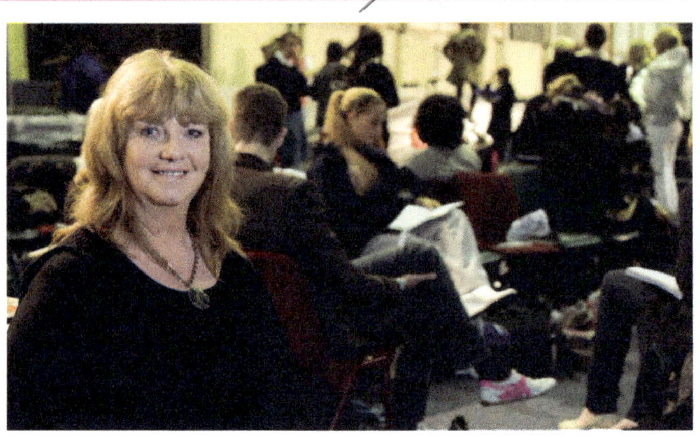

The Competition Director, Heather Palmer, works with garment designers.

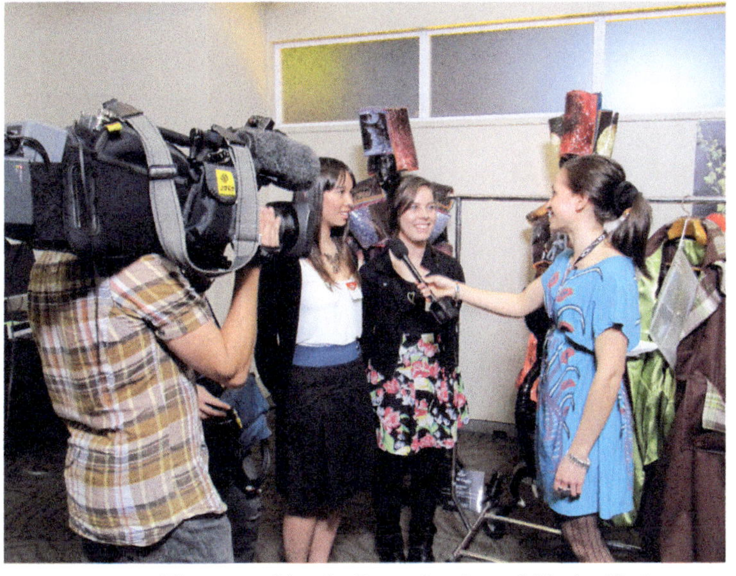

These two friends, Renee Louie and Kayla Christensen, designed and made a WOW garment together. A children's television presenter interviews them about their WOW entry.

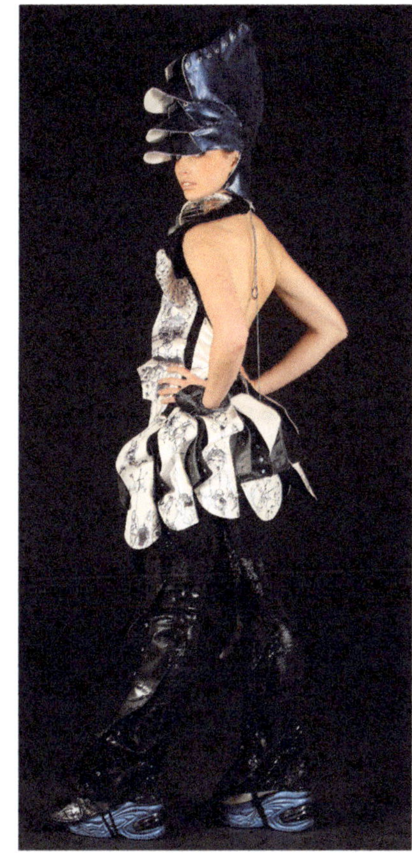

Illustre Shoe-Machine *was designed by Maartje Dijkstra, Netherlands.*

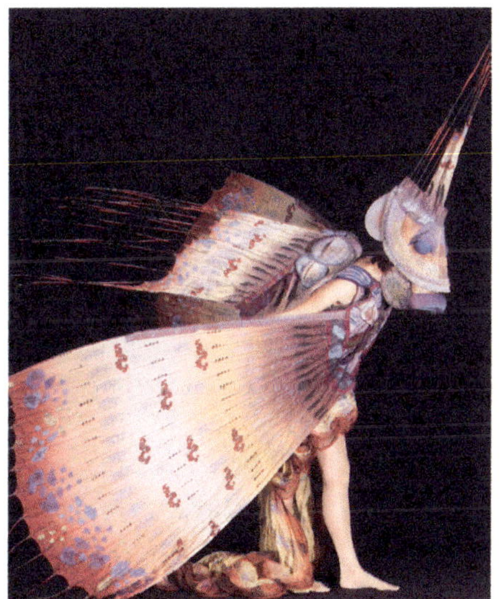

Dragon Fish *was designed by Susan Holmes, New Zealand*

October

After the final shows in October, WOW is over for another year!

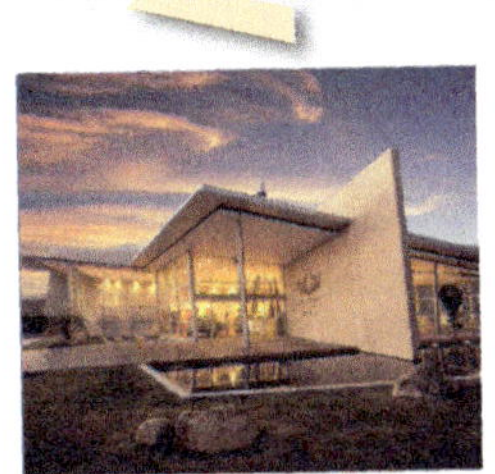

the WOW museum

The WOW garments are repacked for the journey from Wellington back to Nelson – the home of the World of WearableArt Museum.

3 WOW, Creative Excellence!

Enter **Garments** with **Folds**

Designers can enter garments in one of WOW's seven sections. One section is called Creative Excellence. The 2009 theme was Fold and each garment had to feature folds.

Second Skin

This garment was based on a reptile shedding its skin. As its skin lifts and becomes translucent, it makes way for the second skin. Some of the garment's materials were lycra, tulle, nylon and sheepskin.

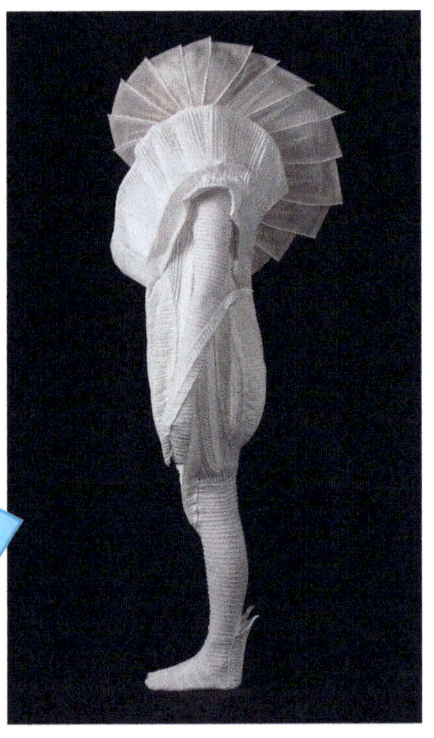

Second Skin *was designed by Hayley May and Fiona Christie, New Zealand.*

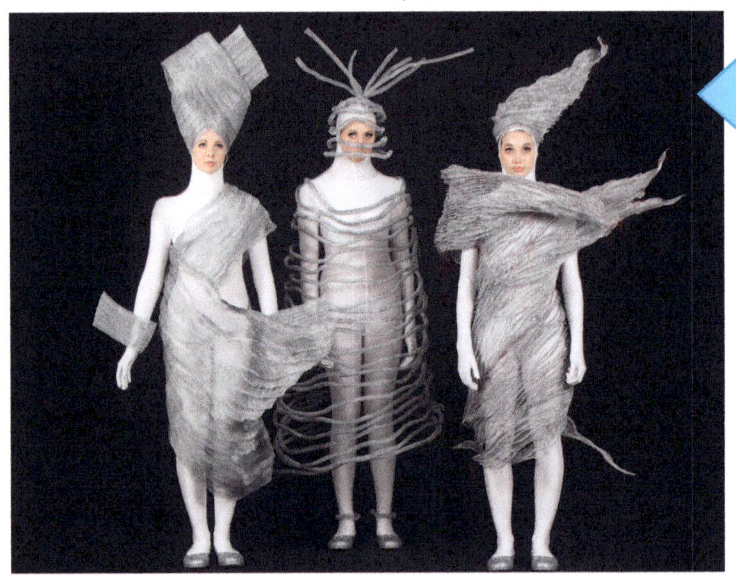

Screen Play *was designed by Amy Jean Boebel and Sue Hobby, USA.*

Screen Play

Aluminium sheeting was the main material used for this garment. The designers were able to fold the thin aluminium sheets and synthetic fibres in many creative ways.

Firebird

This creative garment was inspired by birds of paradise flowers. By using hand-dyed stretch nylon and sticks, the designer created large folds in the wings.

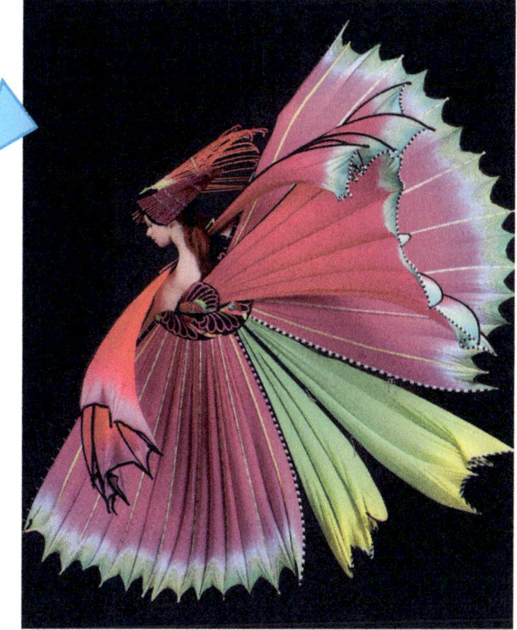

Firebird *was designed by Susan Holmes, New Zealand.*

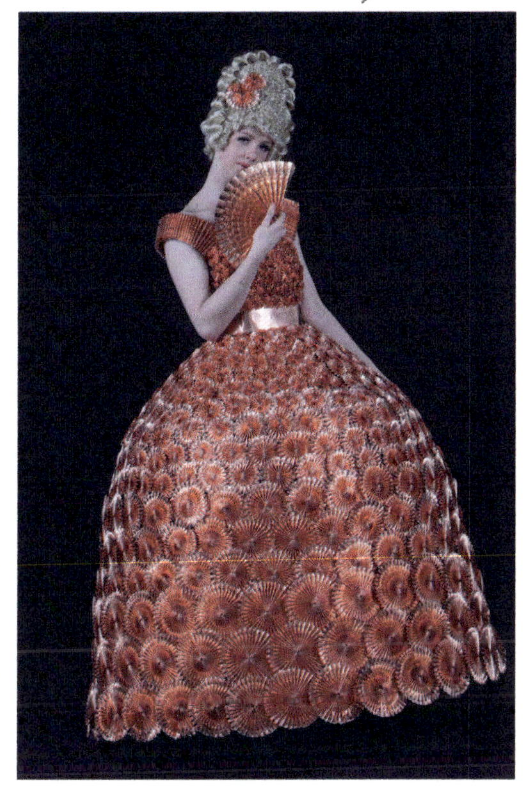

Queen Adelaide *was designed by Emma Whiteside, New Zealand.*

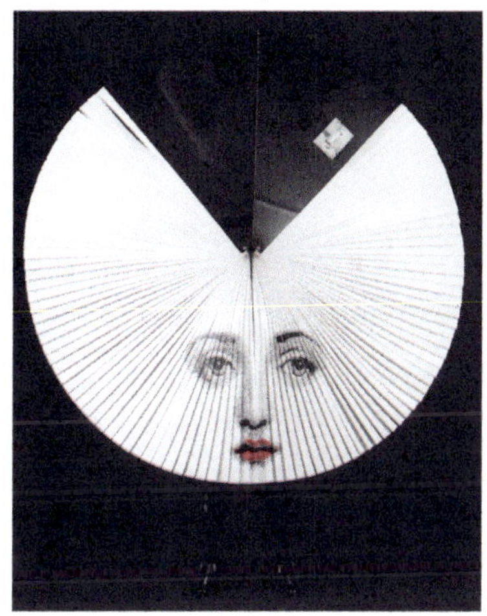

Behind Closed Doors *was designed by Kathryn Preston and Angie Robinson, New Zealand.*

Queen Adelaide

This shimmering garment was a burst of light as the model walked out onto the stage. The main material in the garment was recycled copper that was once used in cars. Aluminium, which is a very light material, was also used.

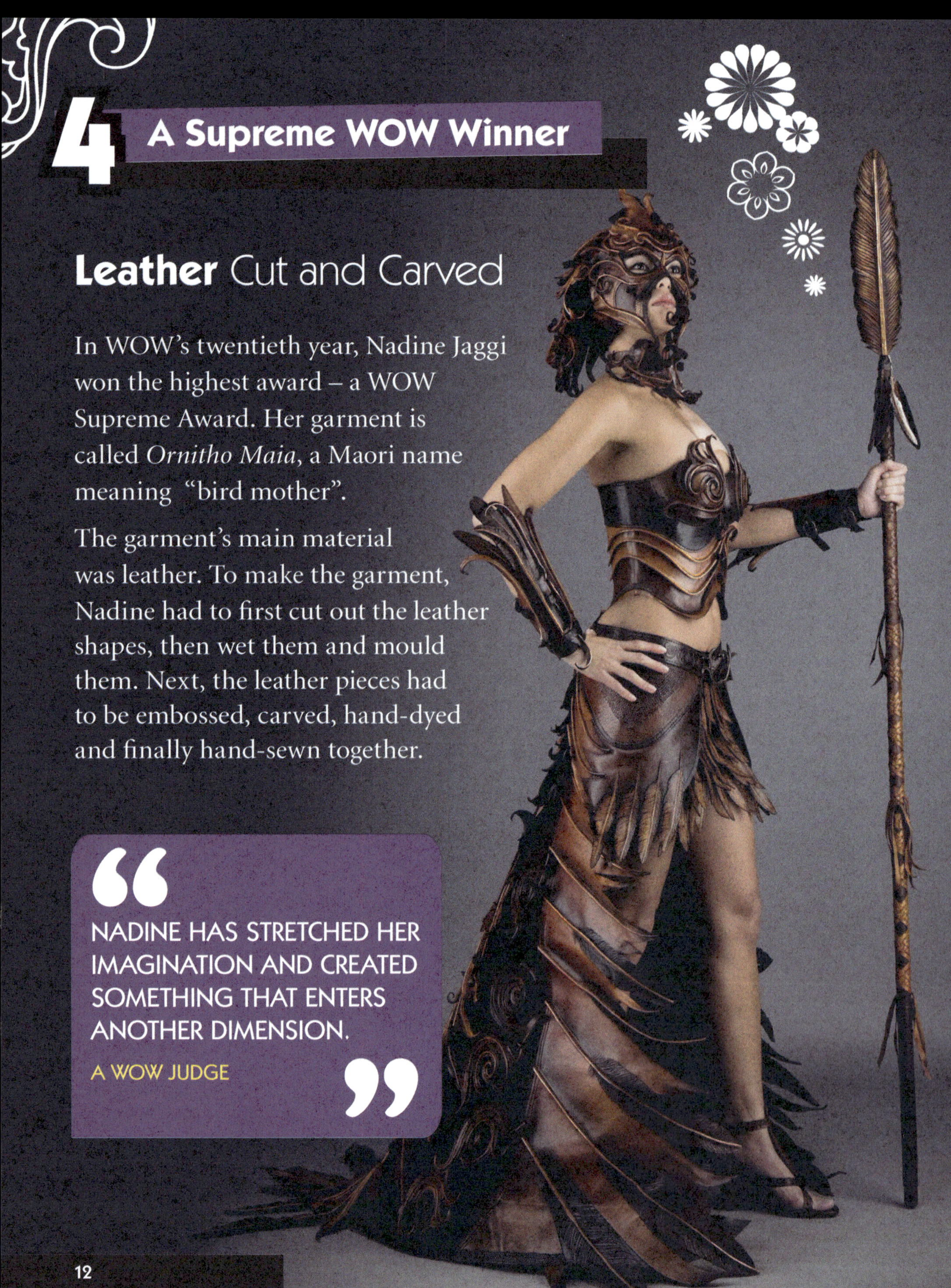

4 A Supreme WOW Winner

Leather Cut and Carved

In WOW's twentieth year, Nadine Jaggi won the highest award – a WOW Supreme Award. Her garment is called *Ornitho Maia*, a Maori name meaning "bird mother".

The garment's main material was leather. To make the garment, Nadine had to first cut out the leather shapes, then wet them and mould them. Next, the leather pieces had to be embossed, carved, hand-dyed and finally hand-sewn together.

> "NADINE HAS STRETCHED HER IMAGINATION AND CREATED SOMETHING THAT ENTERS ANOTHER DIMENSION."
>
> A WOW JUDGE

THE SUPREME AWARD

This is the top award that all designers hope to win! The prize includes money, a trophy and international travel.

Nadine carves part of the garment.

Nadine's Work

Nadine spent many months designing and making her leather garment. Follow some of the stages in Nadine's work as she made this complex garment.

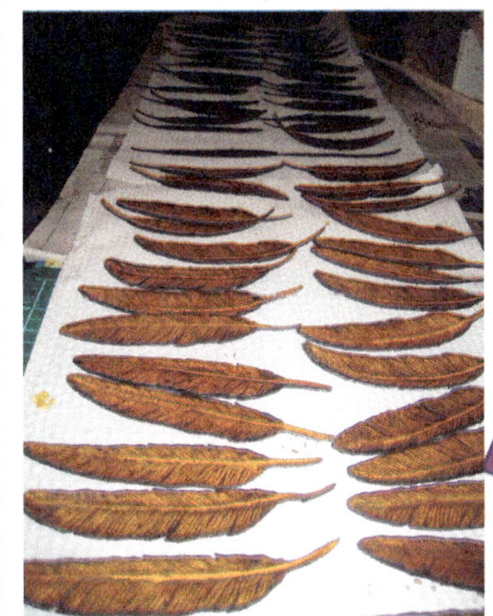

leather feathers laid out to dry

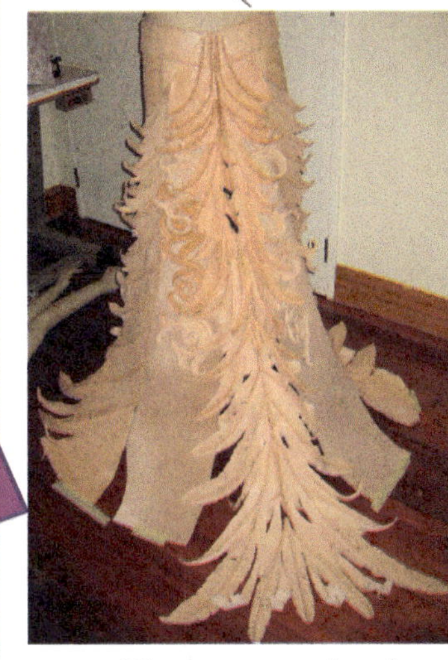

The garment takes shape.

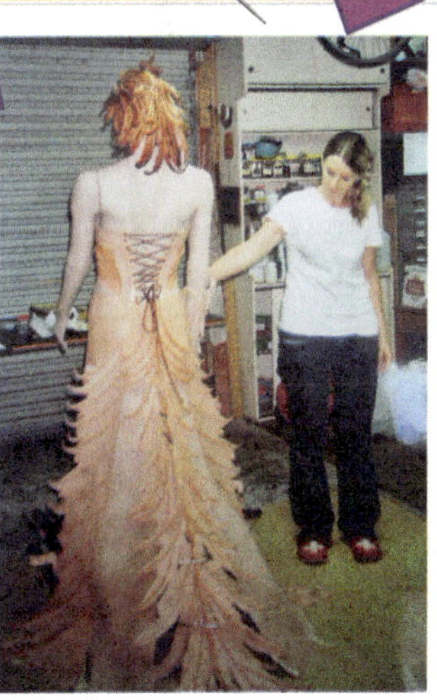

Nadine checks the garment on her mannequin model.

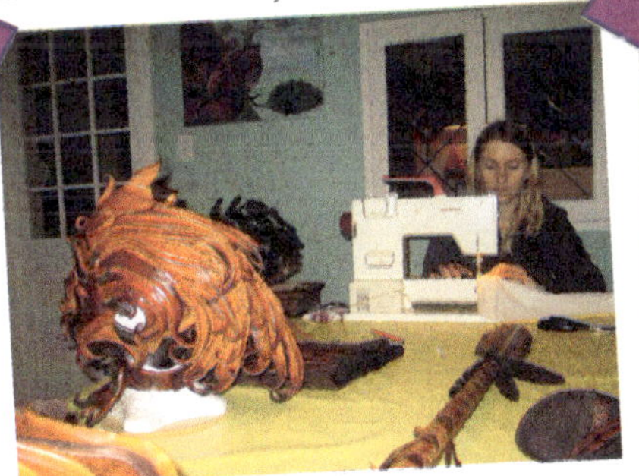

Nadine's garment was hand-sewn. She only used a sewing machine to make storage bags to put the garment in.

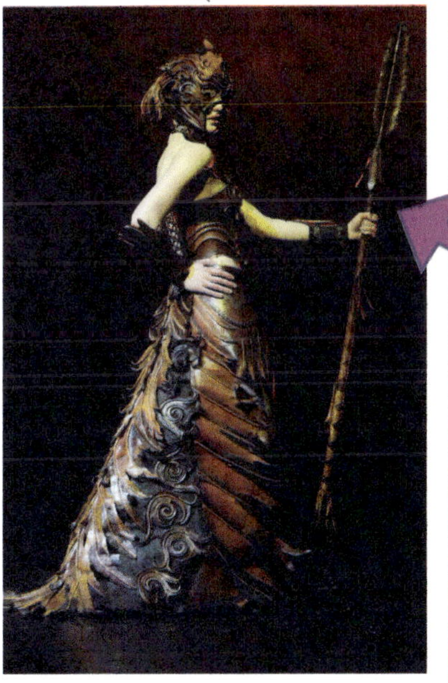

Nadine's garment is modelled onstage at the 2008 show.

5 Claire Wins WOW Awards

TEXT TYPE
Procedure

Claire's First **WOW Entry**

Claire Prebble was only eight years old when she entered her first garment in the WOW competition. It was called *Junk Fish*. This is how she made her first garment for the WOW competition.

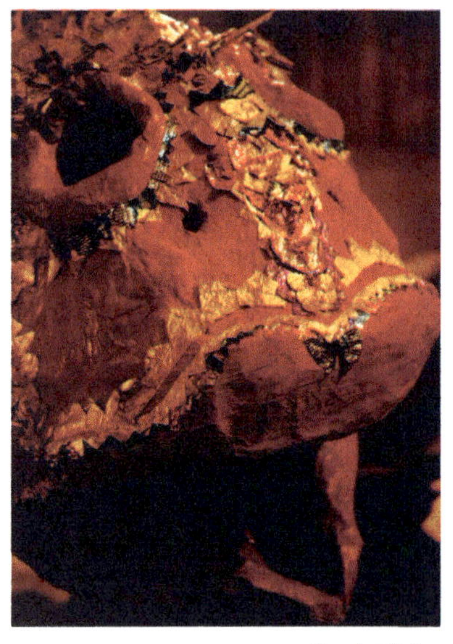
Junk Fish

Junk Fish Materials

- chicken wire
- papier-mâche
- red paint
- lolly wrappers
- chip packets

Junk Fish Method

- First, Claire's mother cut up pieces of chicken wire.
- Then they bent the chicken wire to make a fish-shape frame.
- Next they made papier-mâche.
- Then they moulded the papier-mâche around the wire frame.
- After the papier-mâche was dry, Claire painted the fish.
- Together they cut out shapes from the colourful parts of the lolly wrappers.
- Finally, they stuck the shapes onto the fish and let it dry.

Junk Fish Result

After Claire submitted her *Junk Fish* entry into the competition, it was a finalist in the children's section. Claire enjoyed it so much, she entered a new garment in 13 more WOW competitions. Over that time she has won many awards.

Claire Wins the Supreme Award

In 2004, Claire's tenth garment entry won the highest WOW award. At the time, she was only 18 years old and the youngest person to win the award! Claire's winning garment was called *Eos*. The materials used were sterling silver wire, silk and beads. It took thousands of hours to stitch together all the pieces.

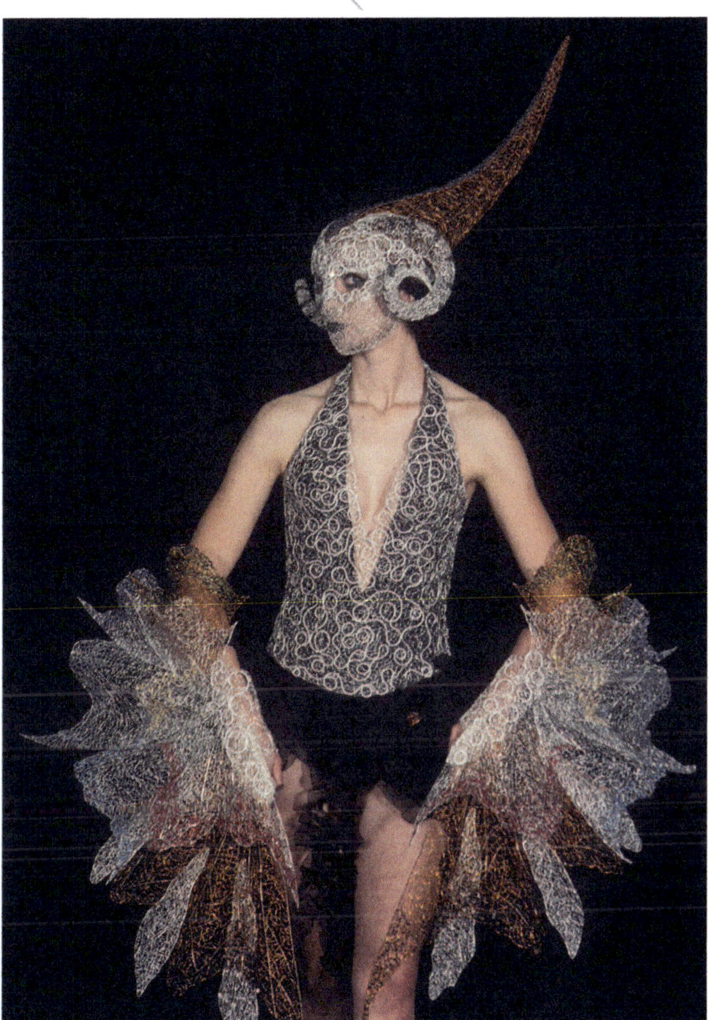

Claire's winning WOW garment Eos. *In Greek mythology, Eos is the goddess of dawn. Claire says, "Eos is a good name, as I worked on this garment for many nights until dawn!"*

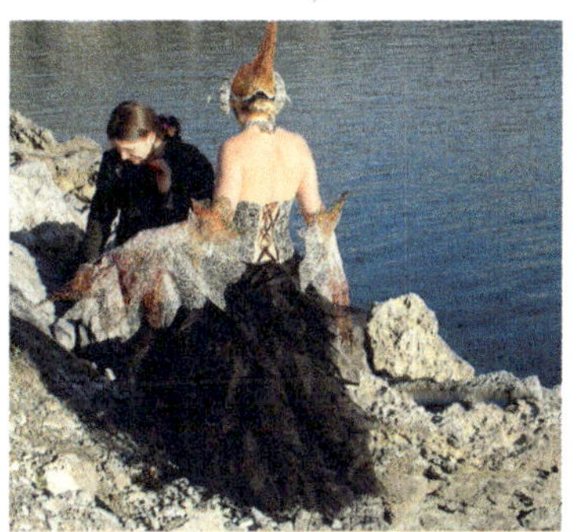

When Claire finished Eos, *she was photographed with the* Eos *model.*

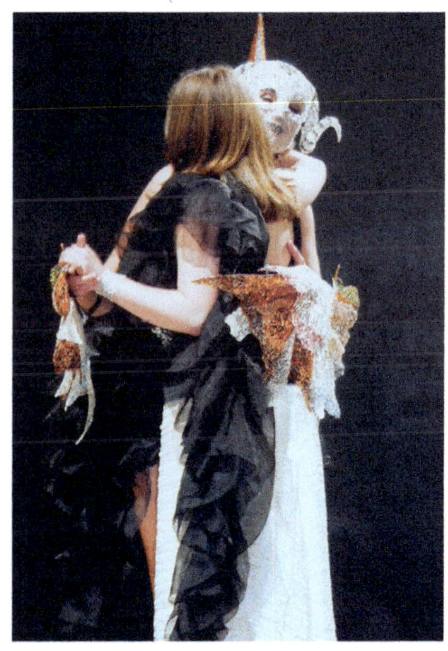

Claire is congratulated onstage for winning the 2009 Supreme Award.

Claire's Live Wire Entry

When Claire was 13 years old, she began working with copper wire to make a garment called *Live Wire*.

WIRE

Claire worked with wire for many of her WOW garments.

Live Wire Materials

- copper wire from an electrical shop
- copper sheets from a craft shop
- stainless steel mesh from a metal recycler
- recycled and new fabrics.

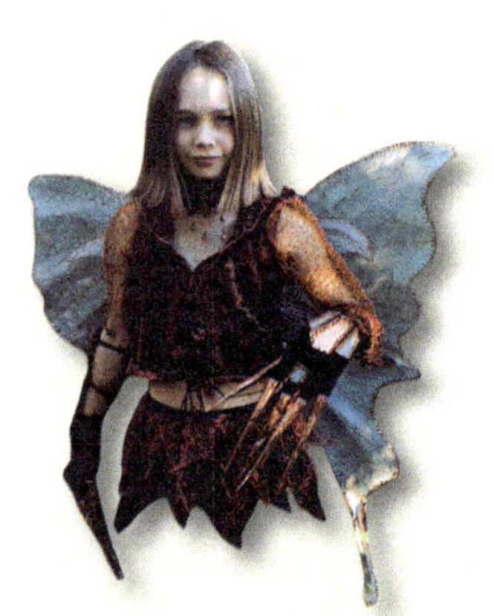

Live Wire Method

To make the garment, Claire:

- cut the copper wire into many lengths
- experimented with the copper wire by knitting small pieces together with different-sized knitting needles
- cut out pieces of fabric and patchworked them together
- sewed the pieces for the stockings
- made a beaded and copper wire necklace
- made wings from stainless steel mesh and copper edges.

Live Wire Close-Up

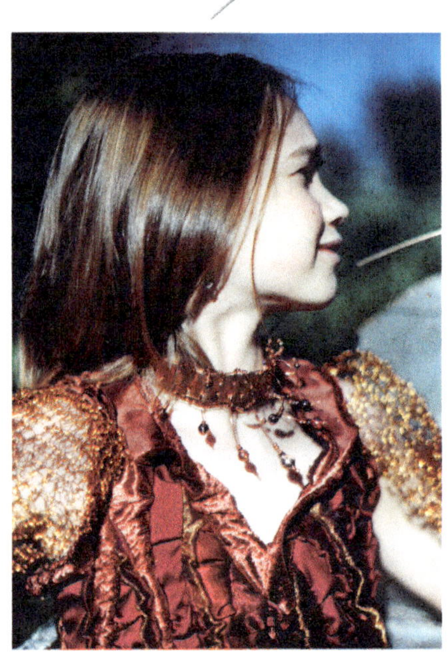

a close-up shows the garment's detail

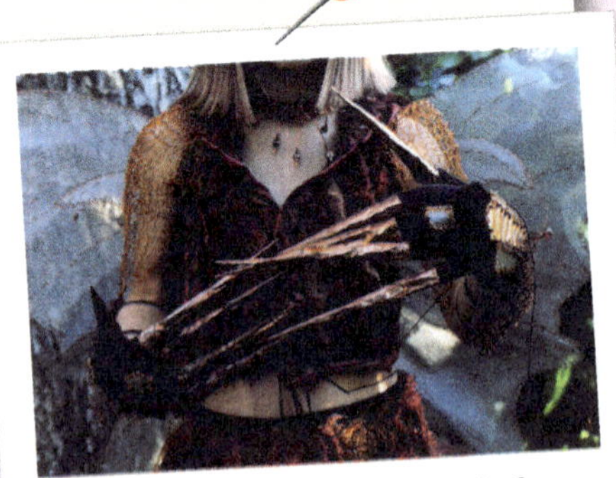

a close-up of the garment's fingers

Live Wire Result

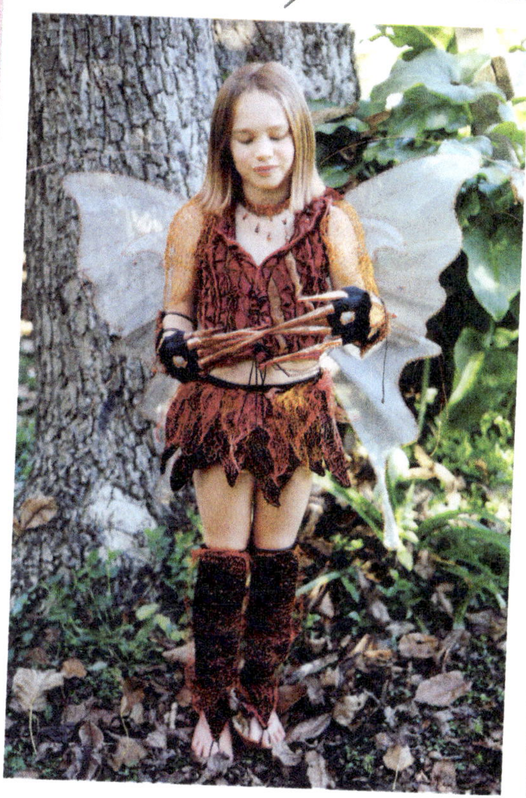

Claire modelling Live Wire

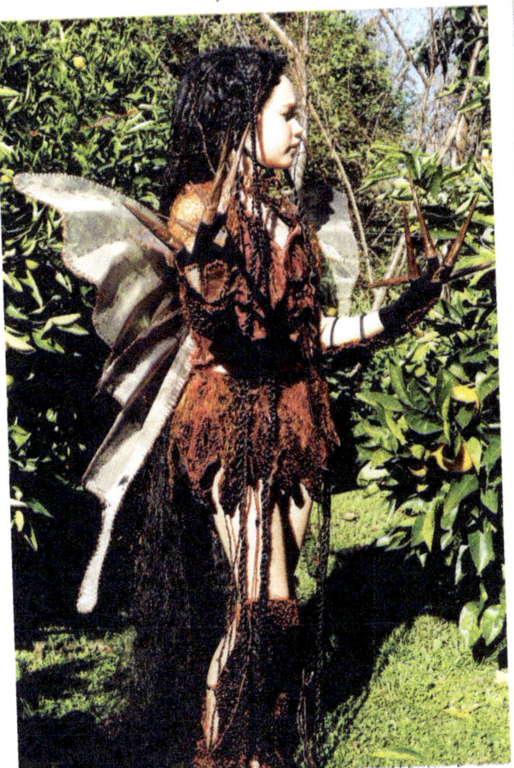

a side view of Live Wire

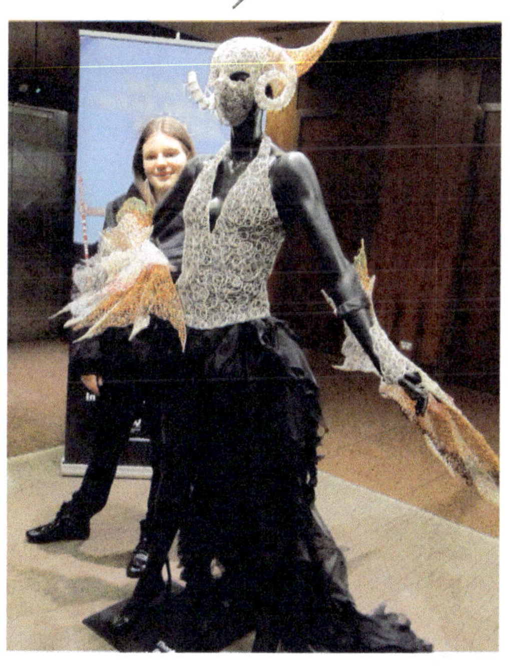

Claire sees Eos *on display during the 2009 show.*

Claire After WOW

Since 2007, Claire has been doing costume construction work for films such as *Avatar*. It took Claire two-and-a-half years to design and make many of the *Avatar* costumes.

Wow, Is That an Illusion?

Illuminating the Illusion

For this section of the WOW competition, designers must create a garment that uses the magic and illusion of UV light. In 2009, the garments for the Illumination Illusion section had to be worn by a model and appear to float, fly or flow above the stage.

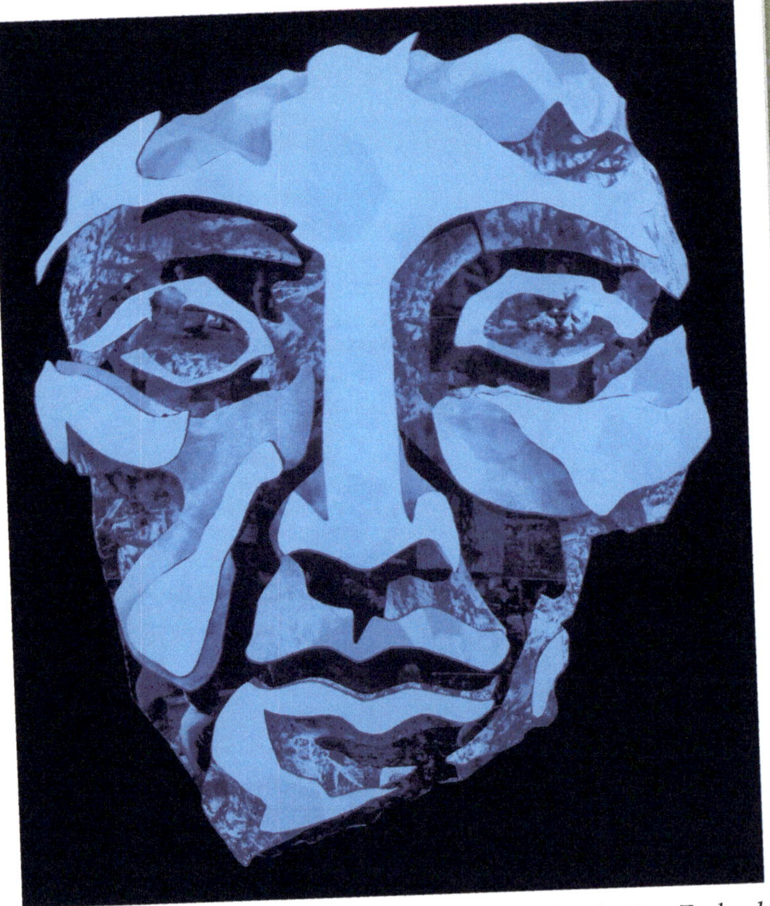

Into Thin Air *was designed by Marie Gant-Roxburgh, New Zealand. It was inspired by old Roman relics. The materials used were foamboard, wood, photocopied photos and MDF.*

UV LIGHT

Ultraviolet (UV) light is light with a colour that cannot normally be seen. In the dark, however, it can make things appear very bright and unusual.

"Float, Fly, Flow" Winner

Wanderer *was designed by Sue Cederman, New Zealand. It was inspired by a Native American legend about butterflies. The materials used were cotton, nylon, paint, netting, wire and paper.*

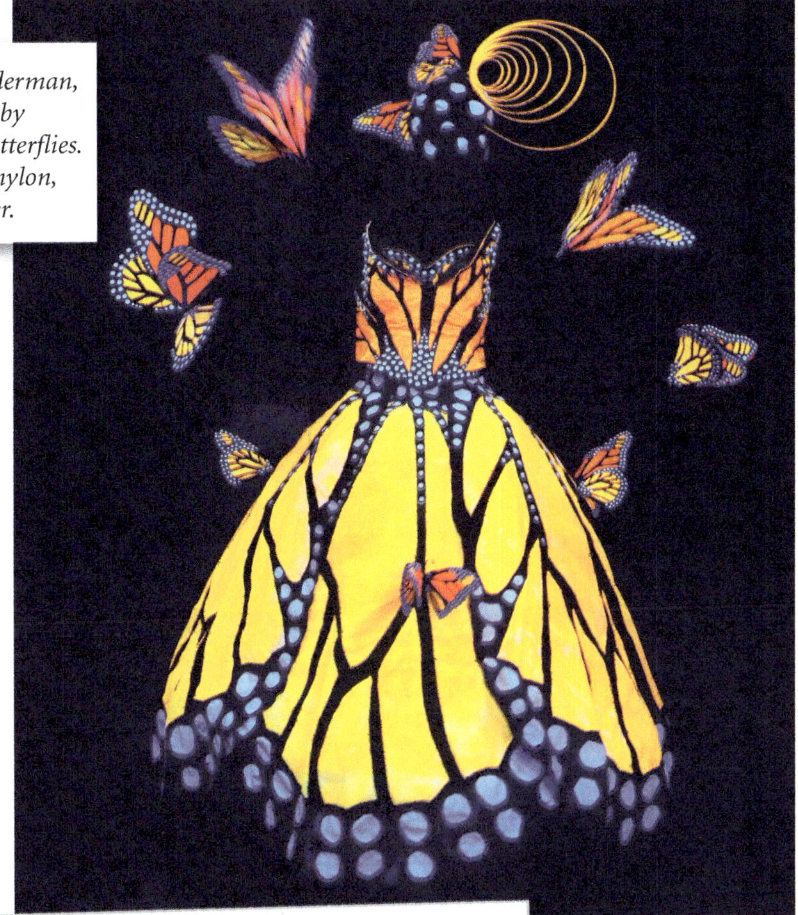

"Float, Fly, Flow" Finalists

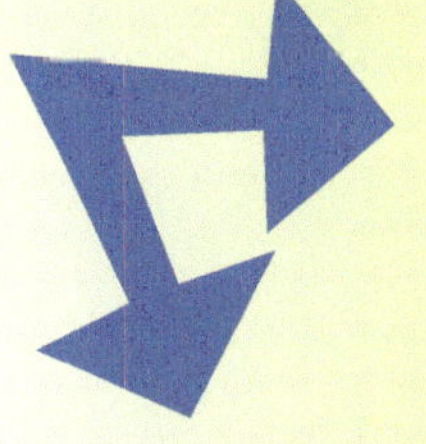

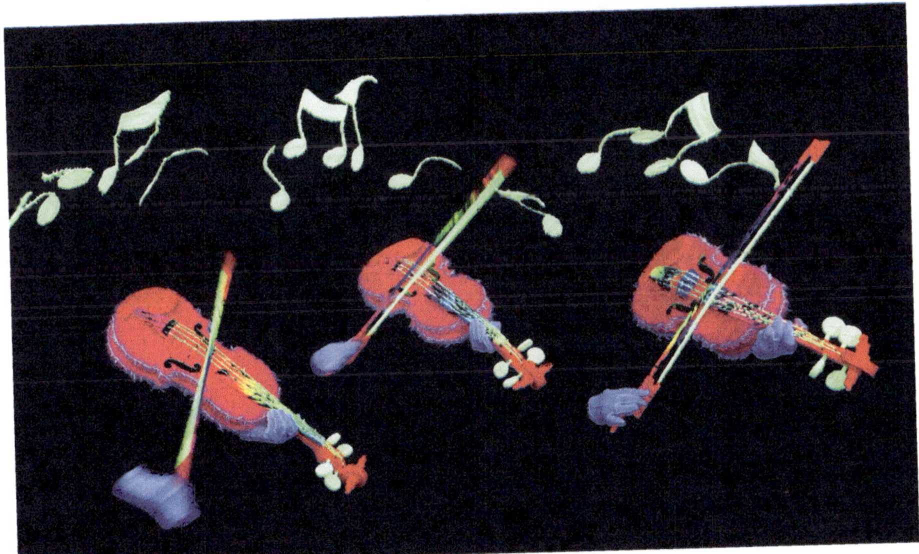

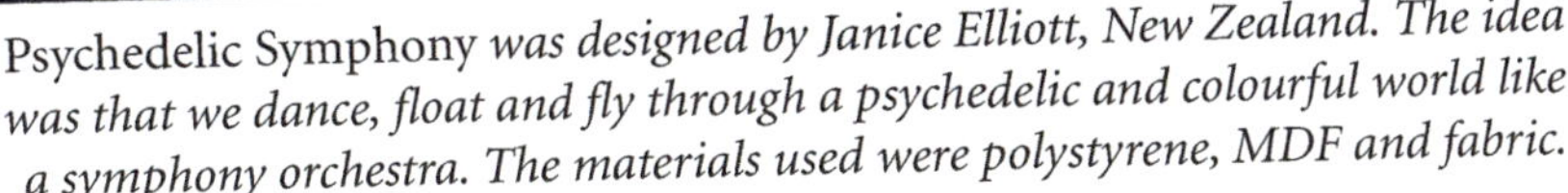

Psychedelic Symphony *was designed by Janice Elliott, New Zealand. The idea was that we dance, float and fly through a psychedelic and colourful world like a symphony orchestra. The materials used were polystyrene, MDF and fabric.*

7 WOW for the Children

Fun in the **Children's** Section

In every WOW show, designers enter garments in the children's section. Each year the theme is different. In 2009, it was "At the Bottom of the Garden". Designers could get inspiration from flora and fauna, insects, ornaments, myths and legends.

"At the Bottom of the Garden" Winner

The idea for this WOW entry, *Dandelion Clock,* came from folklore where the time was told by the number of puffs it took to blow all the seeds off a dandelion globe. The materials used were plastic, fibreglass, foam and fabric.

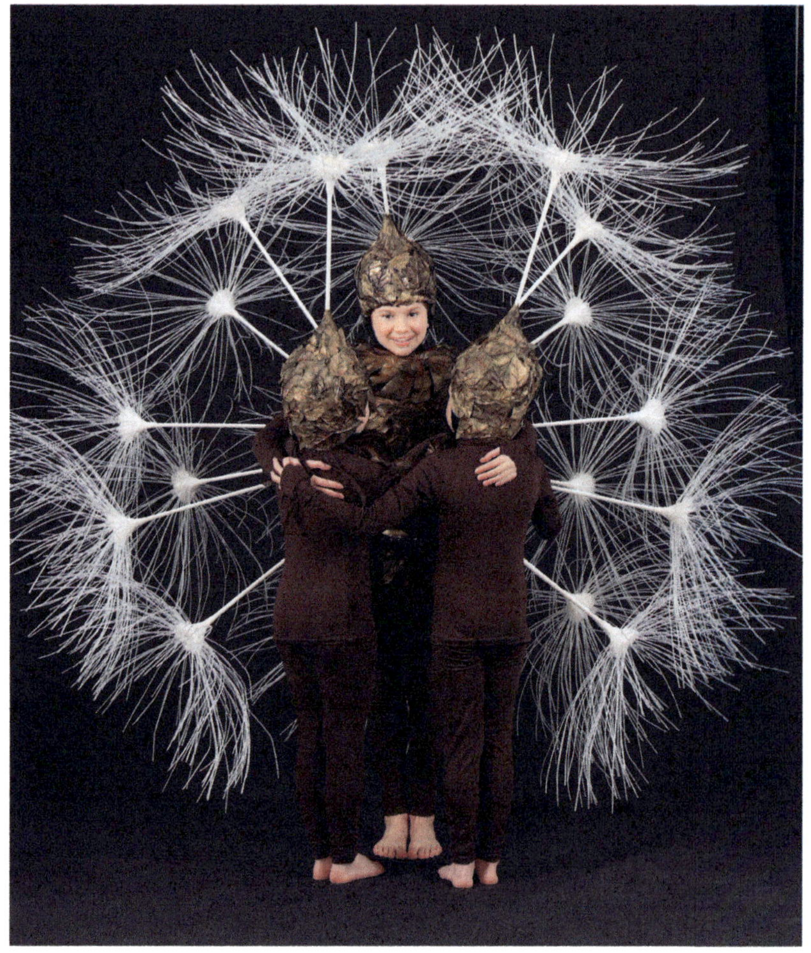

The Dandelion Clock *was designed by Tracey Koole, New Zealand.*

"At the Bottom of the Garden" Finalists

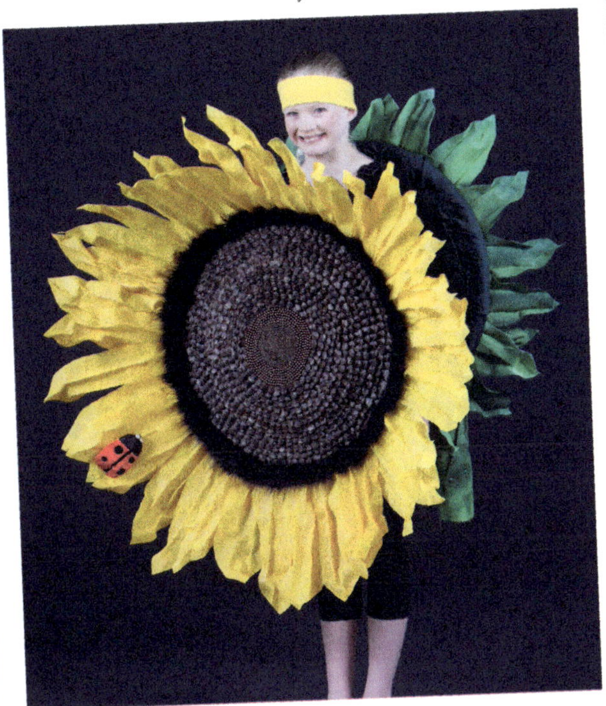

My Big Bloomer *was designed by Paula Rowan, New Zealand. The idea came from her memories of flower shows. The materials used were 900 pine cone scales, fibreglass, beads and polystyrene.*

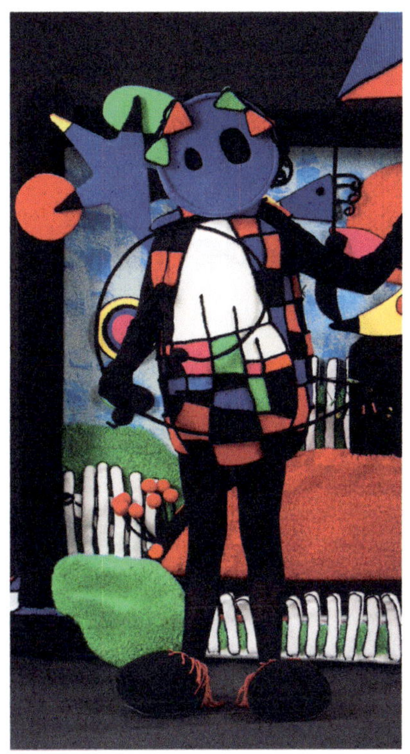

Miro, Miro, Quite Contrary *was designed by Norelle Kendrick, New Zealand. Little Miro wants to see the world but she cannot leave her picture-perfect garden. The materials used were wire, recycled wool, foam, billboards and polystyrene.*

Create Your Own WOW Garments

Imagine your class is having its own WOW competition for the children's section. You could design garments for the same theme, "At the Bottom of the Garden", or you could choose a different one.

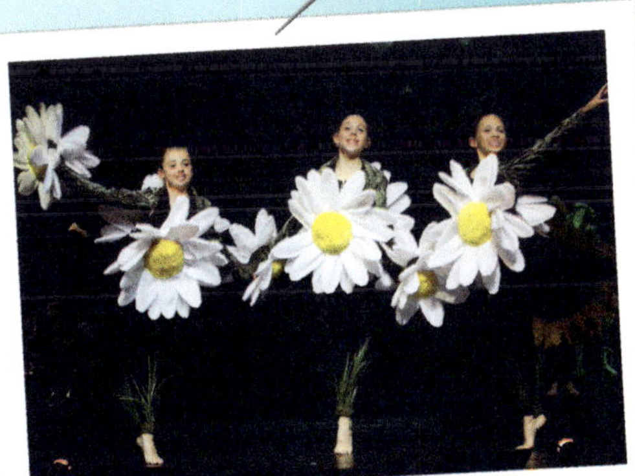

The Daisy Chain *was made of fabric by Virginia Livingstone, New Zealand. The idea was inspired by memories of her sitting with friends, making daisy chains.*

8 More WOW Winners!

A **Carpenter Wins** with Wood

At the 2009 WOW show, a carpenter from Alaska in the USA, won the Supreme Award. David Walker created a wooden replica of a ball gown similar to those worn about 200 years ago.

A Supreme Award Winner

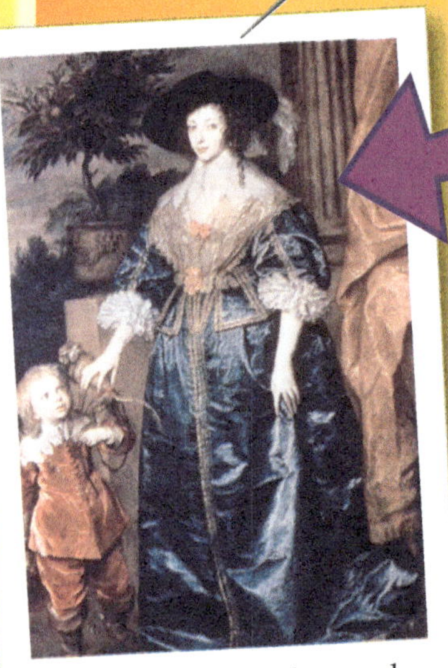

David created a wooden replica of a ball gown similar to this one.

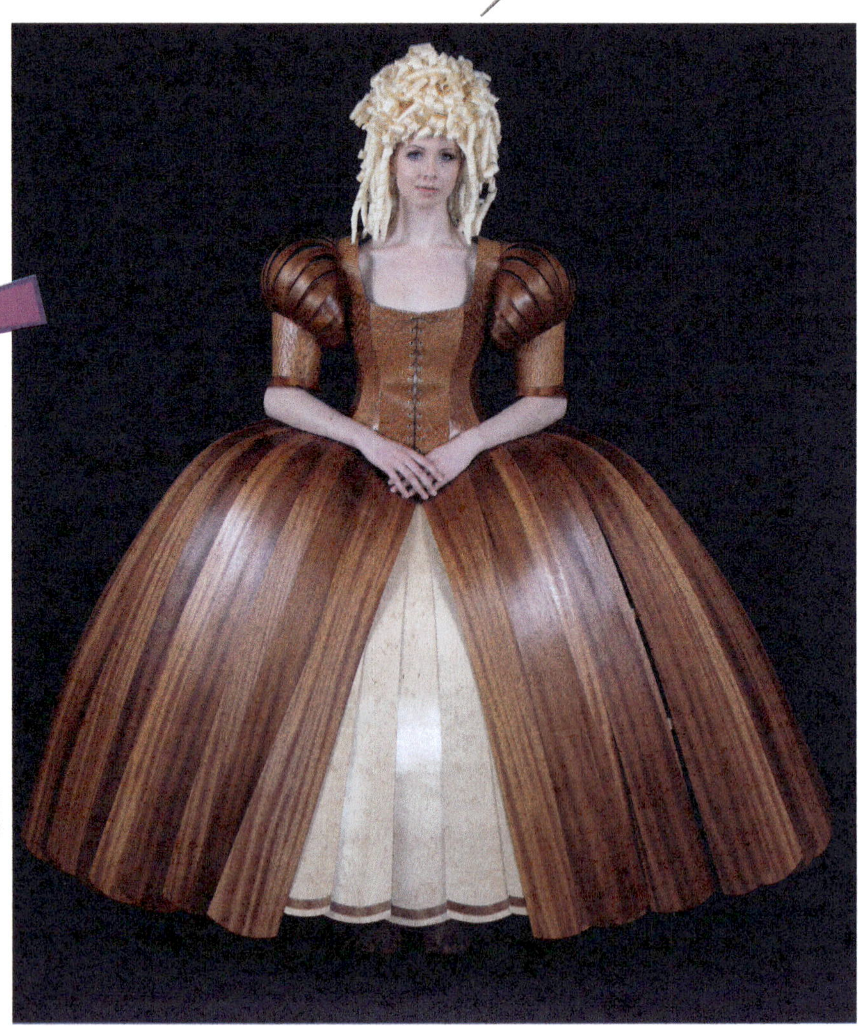

The garment, called Lady of the Wood, *was made entirely of wood. The designer used wood shavings to create a wig of ringlets.*

More Winners

Thousands of designers have created magnificent garments since the first WOW show in 1987. Here are images of some other 2009 winners.

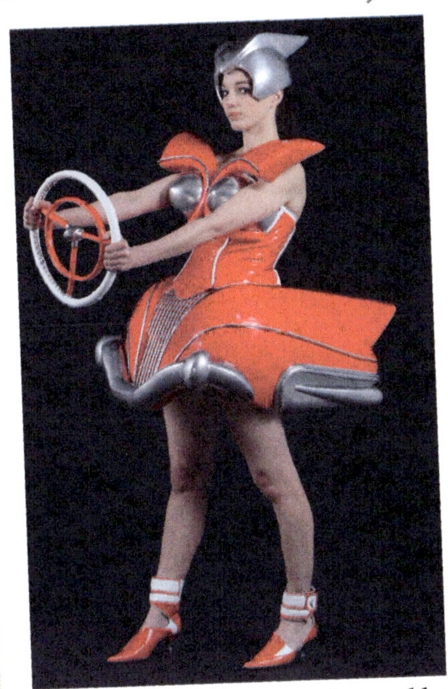

American Dream *was designed by Sarah Thomas, New Zealand.*

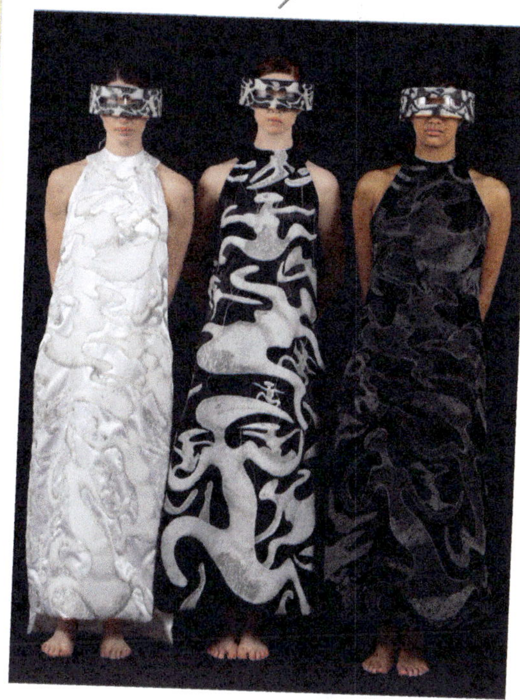

Rock on in the Shadowlands *was designed by Janet Bathgate, New Zealand.*

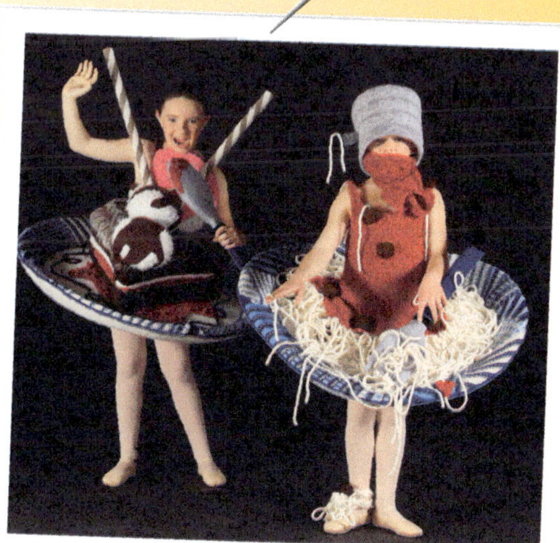

A Song and Dance at Dinner Time *was designed by Norelle Kendrick, New Zealand.*

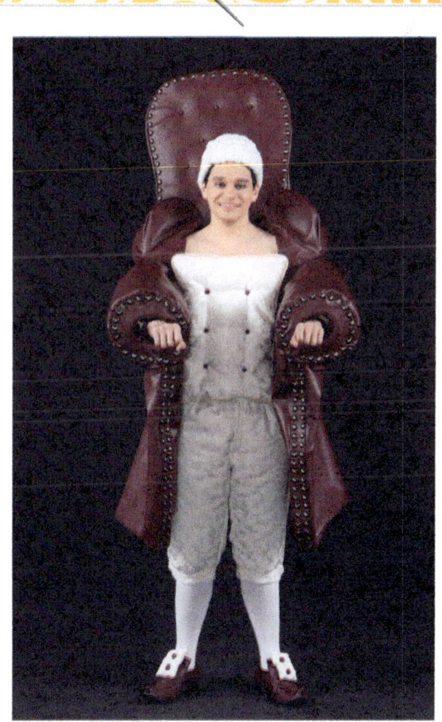

Sir Lazyboy *was designed by Cassandra Bowe, New Zealand.*

Index

Glossary

avant-garde A description for something that is unusual, forward-thinking or experimental

choreography The art of arranging the movements and steps in a dance

dress rehearsal The final practise before a performance, where all the performers wear their costumes

fauna The animals that live in a particular area

flora The plants that live in a particular area

illumination Being brightly-lit

Maori The indigenous people and culture of New Zealand

translucent Able to let light glow through

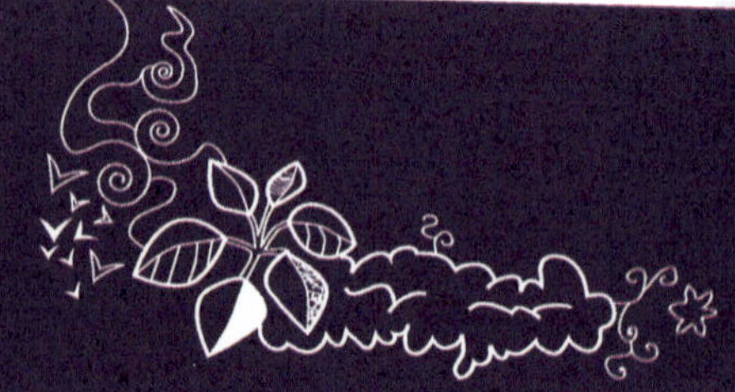